For all the children
we have met

First published in Great Britain in 2003
by Dyscovery Press

Written by Sharon Drew

Illustrated by Peter Adderley

Designed by Simon Dainty

Edited by Amanda Kirby

ISBN 0-9545947-0-3

With an educational grant from Lloyds TSB

Foreword

This charming and magical tale of Jack and Di echoes the experiences of many children with Dyspraxia and other specific learning difficulties such as Dyslexia and ADHD.

Both Di and Jack have felt lonely and desperate at times, and are delighted to know they are not the only ones. They long to be like other children, wanting to join in, but being turned away.

This story highlights the types of difficulties that children with co-ordination difficulties may have. It shows that the child needs to believe in himself, and this then becomes the step on the route to success.

Huge thanks have to go to the many hundreds of children who have told their tale, in order to write this book.

In addition enormous thanks must go to Lloyds TSB; without their support, this book could not have been written.

Amanda Kirby
Dyscovery Centre

Jack and the Disorganised Dragon

 Written by Sharon Drew • Illustrated by Peter Adderley

Chapter 1

The day could only get worse!!!

It had not been a very good day for Jack. Deep in thought he walked along the path heading towards the little wood at the bottom of the lane. His head was bowed low and hands in his pockets, scuffing his feet along the gravel, kicking at nothing as he walked along.

Liam and Toby had been really mean to him at school, calling him names at morning playtime. He didn't want to tell Mrs Lewis, his class teacher, because he didn't want to seem like a tell-tale. And then to top it all he was kept in for the afternoon play, because he did not finish his work in time. Well, at least he escaped Liam and Toby!

Jack liked to go to the woods, especially when he was feeling a bit fed up; no-one could get at him there. Mum always seems to nag at him because he was slow, untidy and was always knocking things over. Harriet, his little sister was just such a goody two shoes, that sometimes he hated her!!

'Don't be long,' his mother yelled after him, 'You know what you're like …no idea of time.'

Jack loved his mum, but he felt sure she didn't understand him.

Dragon Woods was a quiet place. Jack never understood why it was called Dragon Woods, because everyone knows that there is no such thing as dragons. Still, it was fun to think about this as he moved into the undergrowth. He would imagine that he was a brave knight slaying a fire-breathing dragon and saving all the village, instead of feeling like he did, like a wimp with no friends.

Jack looked around. This was a very pretty spot. It was a warm day and the sun was streaming through the leaves making everything dappled as the branches swayed in the breeze. In the spring it was full of bluebells. Jack entered a small clearing. In the middle stood a load of old rubble. Mr Gilby down at number 51 said it was once a hermit's house hundreds of years ago. Legend said, that the hermit used to make spells and potions. Mr Gilby was a kindly old man with whiskers and a wrinkly face.

He looks about 100 years old, thought Jack, grinning to himself, so he would probably remember that it was a hermit's house.

Jack clambered over the stones and found somewhere to sit. Sometimes if he was quiet he could see different animals. Last week he saw a hedgehog and a rabbit.

As he sat, something caught his eye. On one of the big stones was some writing, not graffiti or anything like that, but letters chiselled into the stone. He had been to this spot lots of times but had never noticed it before. Jack looked closer, brushing the moss and leaves away with his hands. He did not recognise the letters. They looked ancient, like the hieroglyphics that he and his class were doing in history.

He could not see all the letters; there seemed to be some drawings on the stone as well. Jack moved his position to try and clear away the smaller stones around it. Maybe he could pull it out to get a better look.

He thought of Toby and Liam, who called him 'rubber band man' and 'Mr Weakling', as he was doing this. 'I'll show them I am not a weakling,' he muttered with some anger in his voice, and with all his strength he tugged at the stone. As he did so, lots of other stones dislodged. There was a big rumble, and Jack lost his balance, and fell backwards. 'Arrrgh,' Jack cried out. All he could remember then was seeing big stones and old branches tumbling towards him.

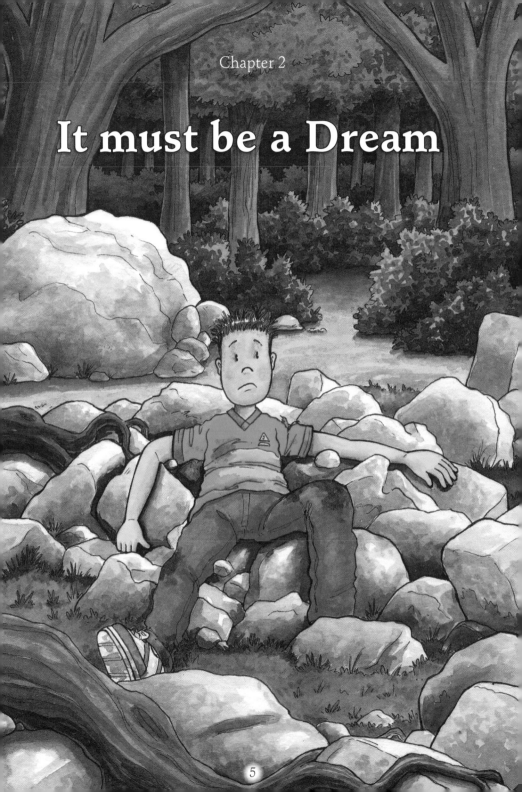

Jack opened his eyes and lay still for a minute. What had just happened? he thought to himself. His mind flew instantly to his mother and the row he would get into - *again!* Was anything broken? Was he bleeding? He carefully moved his arms and legs to try them out. Everything seemed to be in working order. He gently sat up to survey the damage.

'Oooh my head,' said Jack painfully, and reached up to feel a big bump on the side of his head. Then he saw his ripped 'best' T-shirt. 'Oh no,' he groaned out loud, his mother would *definitely* go mad now. Still, he could not see any blood. Breathing a sigh of relief that he had not lost an arm or a leg (not that he was dramatic or anything!!), he looked around.

The sun was still shining and the birds were still singing, but funny, he thought to himself, as he scanned around him, he could not see anything familiar. Jack's heart began to beat faster, he became a bit frightened and he scrabbled to his feet.

'Oooh, ouch,' he said 'My head hurts.'

Not dwelling on this too much, he spun around quickly, desperately looking for something he could recognise. Things were not right, *definitely* not right.

Jack froze to the spot. There was a rustling sound coming from the bushes. He could hear snapping of small branches and twigs. The sound was coming his way. He looked around him for somewhere to hide. He spotted the big stone with the writing on it, the one that caused all his troubles. Oh how he wished he had left it alone. His mother always said that everything he touched went wrong. She was right.

Silently he positioned himself, just like he did when he was watching the animals. He was able to curl himself up quite small. Maybe being a 'rubber band man' had its advantages, he thought, with Toby and Liam in mind. They would never have been able to hide like this.

Now he had a clear view, and waited to see what was coming his way.

As he crouched down, curled up like a ball, he held his breath waiting to see what would happen next. Suddenly Jack thought he could hear someone singing. Maybe, it was Mr Gilby coming along. His heart started to slow; it was alright. Then, into the clearing came a *dragon*. Not a big dragon, not a fearsome dragon, but a dragon nonetheless!!

Jack let out a loud gasp. The dragon looked in his direction. Jack's heart was now beating so fast he thought it would explode out of his body. Oh no, he's seen me. I am going to be eaten for his dinner. Jack was now feeling scared. Should he scream? Would someone come to help him? Somehow he didn't think so.

The dragon moved toward Jack. Jack curled up even more tightly into a ball, thinking if he could make himself small enough, he would disappear. If I close my eyes, he thought, I will wake up and it will all have been a dream. He opened his eyes, no it was not a dream, the dragon was peering right into his face.

Jack didn't know what to do. He just stared into the dragon's big green eyes. Jack was petrified. Any minute now, he will open his mouth, breath fire and I will be burnt to a cinder.

Jack stared with frightened eyes at the dragon. He was about two metres tall and a shiny grey colour. His eyes were the deepest green you had ever seen. Jack began to feel strangely comforted. He could feel the fear draining away from him.

'Well, well,' said the dragon, 'What have we here?' His voice was gentle and melodic.

Jack did not know whether to laugh or be frightened. A *dragon* was hard enough to believe, but a *talking dragon*!!! This is the stuff of books, he thought. Liam and Toby would certainly taunt him even more, if they knew about this.

'What's your name?' said the dragon.

'Jjjjj…..aaaa………..ccckk,' he stuttered.

'How did you get here?' asked the dragon, 'We have not seen a human for hundreds of years.'

'I was in Dragon Wood,' Jack replied, 'I saw a stone with writing on it and wanted to see more of it, so I moved it and now I am here.'

'Dragon Wood!!' the dragon laughed, 'Why is it called that?'

Jack was starting to feel less afraid now. The dragon was not fearsome. He had a kindly face.

Jack told the dragon about the tales he had heard from Mr Gilby. The dragon seemed quite amused by this.

Suddenly, the dragon's face was serious. Jack began to feel afraid again.

'The stone you saw is a magic stone,' the dragon said, 'Only a special person, a very special person is able to use its power. The stone seems to have chosen you.'

'Mm… me….. Mm me…..,' Jack stuttered, feeling like a record that had got stuck, 'Why me?'

'Before I tell you,' the dragon said, 'why don't you come out from behind that stone? You must be very uncomfortable.'

Yes, Jack thought, he was uncomfortable. He was so engrossed with what was happening to him, he didn't realise that his legs had now gone dead. As he stood up, he stumbled and fell towards the dragon and landed on him. The dragon felt warm to touch. His scales were soft. He did not feel slimy or horrible.

Jack was still feeling a little scared. In fact, just now, all Jack wanted to do was cry, just like he did when Liam and Toby were teasing him. But no, he sniffed to himself, I can do this. Oh! This is such an adventure, whether it's real or not.'

'I know a great place where we can go, follow me,' said the dragon.

The dragon led Jack down through the undergrowth. Jack was not sure where he was going, but by this time he thought, I have no choice, let's see what happens.

Chapter 4

What's in a name

Jack followed the dragon along the trail. Neither of them spoke. Jack had to watch carefully where he was putting his feet. He would trip over fresh air , his mother would say. As there were lots of small stones, fallen branches and tangled undergrowth on this path. Jack needed all the concentration he could muster so he wouldn't fall over.

As he picked his way carefully along the path, Jack thought about the other children in his class. He was always amazed when he watched them play: how they were able to run, jump and play dodge and catch, without ever falling over. When Jack tried to do the same, he was always slower than the others, and his arms and legs never seemed to go in the right direction. The girls in his class were kinder to him. But he did not want to seem like a sissy and do girly stuff. The games they played did always seem easier than the ones the boys played.

Jack found that the easiest thing for him to do at playtime, was to do something like helping Mrs Lewis, playing on the computer, talking to the teacher on duty or hanging out by the school fence hoping that no-one would spot him and would come and pick on him.

He thought about Mrs Lewis, his teacher. She was alright, but told him off sometimes for things he did not mean to do, like knocking over the pencil pots or dropping the glue all over the floor in technology. He tried his hardest in class, but his writing especially never looked like the others. It looked like a spider crawling across the page some days.

His most favourite person in school was Mrs Peters. She was the learning support assistant, who took him out of the classroom to give him help in English and Maths. She was great fun to be with and he liked her lessons. However, the other children were starting to call him 'thicko' and 'special needs'.

As Jack thought about this, he resolved that he could not wait to grow up and get out of school. It seemed to be more fun being an adult, he thought to himself, they seemed to be able to do just what they liked.

The sound of a big thud brought Jack back to reality. He looked up, and to his surprise the dragon was flat on his face, with his tail and bottom in the air. His face was covered in mud and a piece of weed dangled from his ear. It was such a funny sight and Jack laughed out loud. In a flash, he felt very guilty and ran to the dragon to see if he was alright.

With a very serious face and a grown up voice Jack asked 'Are you OK?'

The dragon got up in a rather ungainly manner, tottering to the right and to the left.

'Yes, yes,' he said. 'This sort of thing happens to me all the time.'

'Your face is so serious,' the dragon said and burst out laughing. Jack joined in and laughed along with him.

"You looked so funny with your bottom in the air, and with the weeds hanging from your ear,' said Jack. "I am sorry I laughed. The children in my class laugh at me when I fall over and bump into things and it's not very nice."

'I know what you mean', it happens to me all the time' said the dragon quietly and looked sad for a moment. 'Still,' he said, 'it's better to laugh about it; that way the others don't see how you really feel. I find the best thing to do is to just carry on as if nothing has happened. The other dragons say *'Oh it's just Di'.* and they don't take any notice of my clumsy antics, but,' he said with a sigh. 'I would love to be as good as them at doing stuff.'

'Mmmmmm, yes,' said Jack, 'I know what you mean.'

'Di? Jack asked questioningly, 'What does *Di* stand for? Is it short for something or just a nickname?'

'Its short for *disorganised,* said the dragon with a huff. 'Come on,' he said, 'let's just carry on and go to my place.'

Jack stood up for a moment, thinking about the conversation he had just had and how he felt sometimes.

Chapter 5

Clearing out the cobwebs

Jack caught up with the dragon.

'Not far now,' said Di as he pushed past some bushes and into a small opening.

'This is my home. Welcome Jack,' said Di.

Jack blinked his eyes several times to adjust to the light. It was sunny and bright outside and now it was dim and grey. He stood there for a moment and realised he was in a cave. It didn't feel cold or damp, but rather warm and cosy. Sounds didn't echo but were a bit muffled as if there was fluffy carpet on the floor. There was a funny smell; but not one that made your nose turn up, but not one you could give a name to either. The more Jack sniffed the air to try and work out what it smelt of, the more it changed.

Bluebells? – no. Damp grass? – no. Roses? – no.

Anyway, it was kind of pleasant and he wasn't feeling frightened any more. Di seemed a nice sort of dragon.

As Jack's eyes grew accustomed to the light he could see somethings that looked a bit familiar. This is getting more bizarre by the minute. Jack thought. Not only a talking dragon but one who lives in a cave with the sorts of things I would find in my own house.

Jack pinched himself to see if he *really* was not in a dream. 'Ouch,' Jack muttered.

'What was that?" Di asked enquiringly.

'Nothing,' said Jack, trying to keep his voice light, but finding it hard to stifle a bit of a giggle.

Di's cave had table and chairs in it , but it was very messy. There were things hanging out of drawers, pots and plates strewn across the table, old and broken bits of something which Jack could not make head nor tail of in one corner.

'I am beginning to feel quite at home.' Jack said with a chuckle.

'Why's that?' asked Di with a puzzled look on his face.

'This is just like my bedroom at home. **My mother goes bonkers with me, but I just can't seem to make it tidy. My mum is great, but nag, nag, nag, nag, nag, she keeps on and on. We** have tried this and that, but nothing seems to work somehow. Actually, I like it the way it is because I know where everything is. If only she would let me do it *my* way instead of hers.'

'I'd like to be tidy,' said Di, 'but no-one has ever shown me how to or told me some ways that would help. Would you tell me what you have tried? My mother is coming to see me tomorrow, and I would really like to impress her for once.'

Knowing what it felt like to want to do your best, and impress someone, Jack thought how nice it would be to help his new friend. He had never been asked for his advice before and it gave him a warm feeling inside.

Jack glanced around him. 'Uummm,' he mused, 'I don't suppose you have any shops around here, do you,' he said laughingly. 'You can buy some great boxes and other stuff, to help you keep your things tidy. Never mind, we could put some labels or even make some pictures to put on the drawers to help you know what's inside, to start with.'

Jack was pleased with himself for remembering these ideas. Maybe he did listen to his mother after all.

Di and Jack began to tidy up.

As Jack worked, he became lost in his own thoughts. Being organised was not a thing he thought he could do, but actually if he set his mind to it, and worked out a method for himself, he could possibly manage it. Jack smiled to himself; perhaps he could try some of this himself when he got home and make his own room tidier. His mother would be pleased with him for once.

After what seemed like hours, it was finished. Things were sorted into piles, and Di had to choose what he wanted to keep, and what he wanted to throw away. Everything now had a place which would be easier for Di to find things. Jack felt like one of those presenters on the TV, where they go into people's houses and smarten them up before the owners can sell them.

'There! finished,' said Jack looking around him at the very tidy cave. 'Your mother will *definitely* be impressed now Di'

He dusted off his hands and looked down at his clothes. He was filthy. He said out loud to Di 'My mother is going to kill me.'

Di looked around and was very pleased with what he saw.

'This is great. Thank you, Jack, you have been a fantastic help.'

With that, Di reached up to the highest shelf and took down a gold coloured box and gave it to Jack.

'I'd like to give you this, Jack, for all your hard work.'

Jack took the box. He was delighted and surprised at this unexpected gift. The box looked very old. He opened it very carefully. Inside, was a tiny stone dragon with green eyes.

'Oh WOW!' Jack said. 'This is amazing. Thank you very much Di.'

'It was passed down to me by my elders,' said Di. 'It is said that it once belonged to a human who lived here in the woods."

Jack carefully held the stone dragon in his hands and said 'I'll look after it and keep it very safe for you.'

Di smiled to himself and turned away. 'I think we deserve something to eat,' he said 'What about some dinner?'

Chapter 6

Maybe some things are not as bad as they seem

'What do you fancy to eat then?' said Di. He began opening some cupboards and rattling pots.

'Mmmmmm, lets see. I have acorn pie, dandelion bread, thistle soup. My mother is a great cook. She makes them all for me as I am not very good in the kitchen,' laughed Di.

"I can warm things up, but I would not trust myself with a knife. If I pour things out it all ends up on the floor."

Jack was standing in front of Di, watching his movements, listening to his comments.

Why was it, thought Jack, when Di talked about himself, it was like he was describing him. Jack found this strangely reassuring, that perhaps he was not on his own, and that someone else, even if it's a *dragon*, was a bit like him.

'What will you have then, Mr Dreamer?' asked Di.

None of it seemed very appetising to Jack, but he was starving. If he didn't say yes to any of Di's offerings, he knew he would be offended.

'Eerr ummm.' Jack knew that wine could be made out of dandelions so he concluded that maybe this stuff would not be as bad as it seemed.

'I think I will go for the thistle soup,' he announced, hoping that he had made a wise choice.

Don't know why I chose soup, thought Jack, sloppy stuff like that always seems to end up down my front, no matter how careful I am. He glanced down at his clothes. Oh well, my T-shirt is so dirty already no-one would notice any difference. At least I won't have to wrestle with a knife and fork and shoot the food all over the lovely clean table, he thought.

Di put down the soup in front of Jack; to the side was a big chunk of bright yellow dandelion bread. Jack swallowed hard, and thought he was going to be sick. The soup was green, not just a nice green, but the sort of sludge green you would see in a pond that had stood stagnant for a thousand years.

'Yum yum,' said Di, 'come on, eat up, don't let it get cold. My mother makes a mean thistle soup,' and tucked in as though he hadn't eaten for a month.

Oh, how am I going to do this without hurting Di's feelings? thought Jack. He could see Di looking at him. Jack picked up his spoon and stirred the soup slowly.

'Mmmmmm, looks delicious,' said Jack, desperately trying to keep his stomach where it should be.

Di was slurping his soup. This made Jack smile. He did that, but always got told off. Without trying to stare at Di, Jack thought actually slurping is not as bad as all that. Adults make such a fuss about nothing half the time.

'You still haven't tried your soup yet, don't you like it?' said Di with a look of disappointment on his face.

I can't put it off any longer, thought Jack. Perhaps I could say I need to go to the loo or something to get out of eating it. Maybe I could distract Di and pour the soup away somewhere.

Here goes, thought Jack. He stuck in his spoon and took out some of the soup. Oh no! Urgggh, thought Jack, there's something floating in it! Now he definitely felt his stomach in his mouth. In fact it could arrive there at any moment.

I can't get out of it now, Di is watching my every move. Jack closed his eyes and brought the spoon to his mouth. He could feel his hand starting to shake. Keep going, thought Jack, I can't back out now, and with a big gulp, down went the first spoonful.

Jack opened his eyes quickly, and he smiled at Di, who was looking at him with great big green eyes, just waiting to see what Jack thought of his mother's soup. Would he like it or not?

'Faaaaaaaaantastic,' said Jack, very much to his own surprise.

'You see Jack,' said Di, 'sometimes you think things are not going to be very nice or even sometimes you think things are going to be tough, and yet if you have an open mind and go for it, you may be surprised at yourself, and at what you may find.'

'Have some dandelion bread,' said Di, offering him the plate.

'Yes please,' said Jack and tucked hungrily into his meal.

Chapter 7

All in a game

'Di?' Jack paused for a second. 'Where I come from, we don't know much about dragons; we call you mythical creatures. I think it means that you don't really exist. Pictures we have of dragons tend to be big and ugly and breathing fire.' Jack felt a bit embarrassed about saying this, and he could feel his cheeks getting red.

Di laughed loudly. It was so loud, in fact it rumbled around the cave shaking the pots on the shelves.

Jack was relieved that he didn't take offence, and began to laugh as well. Jack was pleased that for once he made someone laugh with him rather than at him.

Di cleared his throat, and looked thoughtful.

'Yes, mmmm, I can see why you humans would think something like that. We have fire-breathing ugly dragons, but that doesn't necessarily make them bad dragons. We have handsome dragons, but that does not make them good dragons.'

'Sometimes we see others who look a bit different, or do things a bit differently, as scary or even a bit odd. But we never even give them a chance before getting to know them. We give up before we even start.'

Di sighed a rather sad sigh, and there was silence for a moment, both lost in their own thoughts.

Suddenly Di said brightly 'I know, there's a game of tail ball down on Unicorn Common. Let's go and see what's going on.'

Jumping up with enthusiasm, Jack followed Di out of the cave and along the track. As they walked along, Jack found himself staring up at the trees to look at the different birds. He looked around at the bushes and leafy vegetation, stopping now and then to inspect some unusual things that he saw. For once Jack didn't trip up over his own feet. Mind you, he had to keep out of the way of Di's tail. He hadn't noticed it before, but it seemed to go in the wrong direction. This gave Di a wobbly sort of walk, which was sort of funny but in a nice kind of way.

'Come on,' said Di, 'we are nearly there.' And with that, the two of them stepped into a wide open space. It was .... Beeeeeeeeeeeeautiful.

From where they stood, you could see for miles. The sky was blue, there were rolling hills in the background of different shades of colour.

Down on the common there was a group of about twelve dragons. Some were about the same size as Di, some smaller, and some bigger. Some were a pinky red colour and some were pale green.

At the end of the common there were markers, and from where Jack stood, they seemed to be hitting an object with their tails.

'It's a bit like football,' shouted Jack excitably, and he started running towards where the game was taking place.

'Wait for me, Jack ....,' shouted Di after him, but Jack did not hear the rest of his words. He was so excited about the sight he saw before him.

As Jack approached the dragons, silence fell. Even the birds seemed to stop singing. You could have heard a pin drop.

The dragons all stopped what they were doing and stared at Jack. Jack froze to the spot.

Oh noooooooo!!! This was not the first time he had felt like this today. He did not move, and they did not move. The silence and the stillness seemed to go on forever.

Thud, thud, thud, down the slope came Di puffing and panting like a steam train, with tail and wings all over the place. The other dragons looked quizzically at Di and then looked back to Jack.

With curiosity, the dragons started to move towards Jack. Jack's heart rate started to race, faster and faster, and fear was again beginning to rise within him. Still there was silence.

'Hi there everyone,' puffed Di, breaking the silence. If Jack had not been so scared the whole scenario would have made him laugh. Jack followed the dragons' gaze to Di.

'This is my friend, Jack,' he said happily. 'He's a human. Don't be afraid, he won't hurt you.'

Jack held his breath and turned his gaze towards the other dragons, waiting to see what their reaction would be. Suddenly the place was full of chatter and laughter, asking questions about Jack. How had Di met him in the first place?

Di put a friendly wing around Jack and said 'See Jack, they have not seen a human before, and they thought you may have hurt them.'

'That's funny.' Jack said, 'I was thinking they were going to *eat me*!!' They both laughed together.

Before Jack knew it, the game had started again, the dragons had lost interest in him and soon the ball was being thwacked up and down the pitch towards the goals, or at least Jack assumed that's what they were.

As the match progressed, both Jack and Di entered into the spirit of the game and cheered and yelled at the players.

During a spell of dull action, Jack said, 'Why don't you join in Di?'

'We talked about this before, Jack,' said Di.

'Yes,' said Jack, 'but you said it didn't matter if you kept falling over and stuff.'

Jack looked at Di's face; he seemed a little sad. Jack thought about how he felt in PE and at playtime and when Liam and Toby wouldn't let him join in. With that thought Mrs Peters also came to mind. Mrs Peters had shown Jack lots of different ways of playing games so that everybody could join in. She made the games fun, and if it went wrong you could just laugh about it. Nobody was made to feel stupid.

With excitement in his voice he jumped up and said, 'I've got an idea. You would like to play, wouldn't you Di?'

'I guess so,' said Di, looking bemused at his new friend.

'Do you think the other dragons would be up for doing something different?' asked Jack enthusiastically.

'I guess so,' said Di, not quite sure where this was leading to. 'We always like new ideas, it can get a bit boring around here sometimes.'

'Well,' said Jack, 'at the end of this game, if you go and gather around the other dragons, I'll show you my idea.'

In no time, the other dragons had been gathered in. Jack stood in the middle, taking control. He stood on a boulder, and spoke

confidently to the dragons. Momentarily, as he spoke, Jack couldn't believe what he was doing. Me, Jack, standing in front of all the dragons!! No-one would ever believe him. He just grinned from ear to ear.

Next, he found himself down on the grass with some of the dragons, showing them what to do. Soon they all joined in, and before too long they were all laughing and having a great time.

Soon the sun started to go down and one by one the dragons had to leave to go home.

'Come on,' said Di. 'Let's get back. It's been a very busy day. I have had a great time, and for the first time I felt I could join in and be the same as everyone else.' He paused for a moment. 'Jack, you were very impressive back there, you know. You were great at showing others what to do and encouraging them to play and join in. Mind you,' he said with a chuckle, 'Your catching sucks.'

Jack was touched by this speech and blushed at the praise. He smiled at Di's joke. With that, he picked up a muddy clod of grass and threw it at Di, and ran away laughing.

'Yeh,' he yelled back at him, 'But my aim's not so bad is it?'

Di stood there for a moment smiling, and for the second time today had things sticking out from his ears.

Chapter 8

Was it a dream?

Jack and Di walked slowly back to the cave, chatting about this and that as they went, and both feeling quite tired but happy.

'I could eat another bowlful of your mother's soup,' Jack said.

As they walked, Jack suddenly found he recognised where he was. It was the clearing where he and Di had met this morning.

'Look,' shouted Jack, There's the stone with the writing on; you still haven't told me what it means.'

With that, Jack started to run over to the stone. So intent on where he was going, he did not hear Di calling after him, nor did he see the root of a tree in front of him. He stumbled right over it. Forwards he went, as if he was shot out of a cannon. His hands were outstretched in front of him like Superman flying through the air. The last thing he remembered was seeing a big old tree looming up before him and his head was aimed right at the trunk.

Jack opened his eyes, and lay where he was for a minute. What had just happened? he thought to himself. Was anything broken? Was he bleeding? He tentatively moved his arms and legs to test them out. Everything seems in working order he thought, and gently sat up to survey the damage.

'Ooogggh, my head,' said Jack painfully, and reached up to feel a big bump on the side of his head. Then he saw his ripped T-shirt.

'Oh no,' he groaned out loud. His mother would go mad. Still, he could not see any blood. Breathing a sigh of relief that he had not lost an arm or a leg (not that he was dramatic or anything!!), he looked around.

The sun was still shining and the birds were still singing.

He recognised this was a familiar place. He was in Dragon Woods. But his head was throbbing. One of those big stones must have hit him.

Jack was just about to get to his feet, but then froze to the spot. There was a rustling sound coming from the right. He could hear snapping of small branches and twigs. The sound was coming his way. Frantically, he looked around him for somewhere to hide. He spotted the big stone with the writing on it, the one that was the cause of all this trouble. Before he had time to get up, he realised that somebody was behind him.

'Are you alright Jack?' said a voice. Jack looked up, and with relief saw it was Mr Gilby.

'Yes, yes,' Jack said, words stumbling out of his mouth.

As he stood up, flashes of images came flooding back.

Was it all a dream?

'I found a stone with interesting writing on it, and tried to pull it out to get a better look. But I think I must have fallen and bumped my head.'

In a quiet voice and with a knowing twinkle in his eye, Mr Gilby said 'Didn't see any dragons… did you?'

'Er, uh mmm,' was all Jack could mutter.

'I know,' said Mr Gilby gently, and with that, put a hand on Jack's shoulder.

'Best get off home now, Jack, and let your mum see to that bump on your head.'

'Yes,' said Jack, and walked slowly away from the clearing. Jack glanced back and saw Mr Gilby still standing where they had parted, smiling. It was as if he knew something, thought Jack.

Jack walked up the lane towards his house. He was filthy. Suddenly he became a bit nervous. How long had he been gone? Had he missed his tea? Was his mother out looking for him? Oh boy, I'm in trouble again he thought.

He quickened his pace. Somehow, he felt different though. He didn't know what, but something had happened to him back

there in Dragon Woods. Images came flooding back: Di, the cave, the football match, teaching others different games.

He opened the back gate and guiltily crept up the path.

'Oh there you are, Jack, I was beginning to wonder where you were.' There was his mother hanging out the washing on the line. Sheer relief washed over him. Mind you, she had not seen the mucky state he was in...... yet.

Quick as you can, thought Jack, get in the back door and up the stairs before..........

'Good grief Jack,' said his mother in an exasperated tone. Jack froze to the spot. He seemed to be doing this a lot today.

He waited. Here it comes he thought.

'How on earth did you get that dirty?' she asked. 'Still, I suppose I should never be surprised with anything you do. Go upstairs and put those dirty things in the wash basket and clean yourself up ready for tea.'

In his bedroom, he looked around him. It *was* messy and he could see why his mother got cross with him. His thoughts floated back to Di, and he said out loud to no one in particular, 'If I did it for Di, then maybe I could start to do it for myself. I'll give it a go after school tomorrow. I'll give Mum a nice surprise.'

He started to undress. Jack thought he had been away for a lifetime, but nothing had changed at all, or had it?

Hopping about on one leg, he finally pulled off his trousers and on to the floor fell a tiny object.

Jack bent to pick it up. It was a beautiful tiny dragon with green eyes. Jack held it for a moment and he thought of Di. He carefully placed it in his secret box in his cupboard where he kept all his special things, and smiled to himself.

Perhaps, it wasn't a dream after all.

The End

The Dyscovery Trust

The Dyscovery Trust was set up in 2000 to raise awareness across the UK with regard to Dyspraxia also known as Developmental Co-ordination Disorder.

It aims to:

- Disseminate information to health and educational professionals.

- Support parents and their children by increasing their understanding of the condition.

- Produce suitable educational materials and practical tools.

- Research into the cause of Dyspraxia and related difficulties.

For further information about the work of the Trust go to
www.dyscoverytrust.org